Ready for takeoff?

Title: The Adventures of AeroSquad: Robbie Raptor and the Invisiloop

Author: Taylor Fox

Publisher: Amazon KDP

ISBN: 979-8-9882483-1-6

First Edition

Published: September 2023

For jet facts at the end of the book, data derived from:
U.S. Air Force. (2022, August). F-22 Raptor. Retrieved from https://www.af.mil/About-Us/Fact-Sheets/Display/Article/104506/f-22-raptor/.

Project Designer: Celina Milla

For inquiries regarding permissions or to contact the author, please write to:

www.AeroSquadKids.com

For the original Wingkids,
Liam, Mikey Steves and Noli Boccioli

The Adventures of AeroSquad
Robbie Raptor
& the Invisiloop

By Taylor Fox

Robbie Raptor was a daring little fighter jet. He spent most of his days flying with his squad, going on secret missions, and saving the world from danger.

The AeroSquad included Pedro Panther, Wiley Warthog, Vicky Viper and other amazing jets. They were all great wing-buddies and always had each other's backs.

Robbie was a very special fighter jet because he could fly at supersonic speeds AND become invisible to radar with his stealth mode. Whenever Robbie needed any of his special powers, he would simply yell,

"Afterburners Engage!"

This would activate his stealth mode, and his little engines would fire up, launching him into the stratosphere. Secret missions were his specialty.

But when it came to playing with his friends, they never appreciated his special powers. He could do amazing things, but nobody ever seemed to notice.

One morning, the squad decided to play one of his favorite games in the world – racing.

"Let's see who can really fly the fastest and highest!" yelled Vicky from afar.

Robbie was excited.

"Look what I can do, guys!" he whooped.
"Afterburners Engage!"

Like *Magic,* Robbie vanished into the clouds as he climbed at supersonic speeds. He was almost reaching the top of the stratosphere when he heard cheering in the distance.

"One more victory for Vicky Viper!"

The squad cheered because they had lost sight of Robbie.

Robbie was heartbroken. His clear win had gone unnoticed. He turned off his stealth mode and glided back to the team, his engines whining at idle.

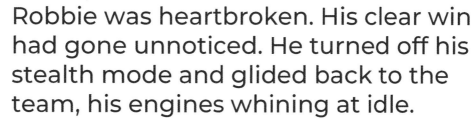

"Where were you, Robbie?" They asked.

A low-spirited Robbie replied, "I was just...
nevermind. Congratulations, Vicky."

Robbie sighed as he returned to home base, feeling alone. What is the point of being special if you can't show your friends?

Papa Jack, the old biplane, heard some sniffles coming from the hangar, so he taxied over to find the young Raptor tearing up.

"Aw, it's okay Robbie. What seems to be the problem, kiddo?"

"Why do I have this stealthy superpower if nobody can see me use it?

Sometimes I feel like I am invisible."

Papa Jack smiled lovingly. "I understand how you feel, Robbie. You want your friends to see your superpower, but it's still a superpower even when no one is watching.

You are amazing even if they don't see it.
Many heroes go unnoticed everyday."

Robbie's eyes widened. Papa Jack was right.

Just as the last sentence left Papa Jack's mouth, he and Robbie heard a scream.

"HelllPPP!" The AeroSquad was in trouble.

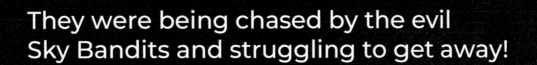

They were being chased by the evil
Sky Bandits and struggling to get away!

"Not on my radar! Afterburners Engage!" yelled Robbie as his engines roared to life and he shot straight up into the sky.

Skoooooooouup!

Robbie's stealth mode allowed him to go unnoticed by the Sky Bandits. When he arrived at the scene, he took everyone by surprise.

"Stay away from my friends!" he yelled. He accelerated in front of them and created a huge sonic boom as he broke the sound barrier and performed his famous **INVISILOOP** around the mean jets!

Shhhhhheewwww Kabooooom!

The shock wave from the sonic boom made the Sky Bandits spin out of control. Confused, they quickly bugged out once they could fly again.

Robbie!" yelled the squad. "That was amazing! We never saw you coming!"

"Oh, my stealth mode was on," Robbie winked.

The AeroSquad rejoined for their heroic flight back home and everyone praised him, chanting,

"Robbie! Robbie! Robbie!"

That day, Robbie learned that real superheroes save the day, even when no one is watching. He had great friends who appreciated him, but their cheer wasn't the only fuel his little engine needed.

Being proud and loving himself was just as big of a superpower as being stealthy and invisible.

The End.

Photograph by: Bill Fauth

F-22 Raptor

Robbie Raptor is based on the F-22A Raptor. The Raptor is a super-fast and stealthy jet fighter plane. It has a sleek and futuristic design, capable of flying at incredible speeds and outmaneuvering other aircraft. The Raptor is equipped with advanced sensors and weapons, making it a fearsome air-to-air combatant. Its primary mission is to dominate the skies and provide air superiority.

Max Altitude:
50,000 feet +
Almost twice as high as a passenger jet can fly!

Wingspan:
44' 6" (13.6 mts)
The size of a humpback whale.

Max Weight:
83,500 lbs
Like 7 African elephants!

Height:
16'8" (5.1 mts)
Same height as a giraffe.

Thrust:
70,000 lbs
How many pounds can you push?

Fuel Tank:
18,000 lbs
2,686 gallons, like filling up a car 179 times.

Length:
62'1" (18.9 mts)
About the same length as a bowling lane.

Top Speed:
1,500 m/h
Mach 2, twice the speed of sound!

Cost:
$143 million
Like buying 715,000 bicycles!

First Flight:
Sept 1997
Same year Harry Potter was published.

Fun Fact!

Did you know that fighter jets are so fast they can fly faster than the speed of sound? When they break the sound barrier, they create a loud 'boom' called a sonic boom that can even break windows in a house! So, next time you hear your mom asking you to come to dinner, just remember, the sound of her voice is much slower than these incredible jets!

How Good are your Pilot eyes?

1. Did you notice a cloud animal anywhere? What animal was it?
2. Pilots have to watch out for birds! How many birds did you see in the book?
3. Sammy Strike Eagle always wears his famous Starglasses, did you notice anyone else trying them on?
4. In every story, we include a real life fighter pilot callsign (nickname) of someone that flew with author Taylor. Can you figure out which word it is?
5. Robbie is an F-22 fighter jet, did you notice the number 22 in the book?
6. Did you spot the AeroSquad wing emblem anywhere?

Find answers at the bottom of page 37!

CHARACTER SKILL CHART

Robbie Raptor (F-22)

Speed	Air support
●●●●●	●●●●○
Stealth	Ground Support
●●●●●	●●○○○
Maneuverability	Endurance
●●●●●	●●●○○
Versatility	Sensors
●●●○○	●●●●○

Wiley Warthog (A-10)

Speed	Air support
●●○○○	●●●○○
Stealth	Ground Support
●●○○○	●●●●●
Maneuverability	Endurance
●●●○○	●●●●○
Versatility	Sensors
●●●○○	●●●○○

Vicky Viper (F-16)

Speed	Air support
●●●●○	●●●●○
Stealth	Ground Support
●●○○○	●●●●○
Maneuverability	Endurance
●●●●○	●●●○○
Versatility	Sensors
●●●●●	●●●●○

Harry Hornet (F-18)

Speed	Air support
●●●●○	●●●●○
Stealth	Ground Support
●●●○○	●●●●○
Maneuverability	Endurance
●●●●○	●●●○○
Versatility	Sensors
●●●●●	●●●●○

Pedro Panther (F-35)

Speed	Air support
●●●●○	●●●●●
Stealth	Ground Support
●●●●●	●●●●○
Maneuverability	Endurance
●●●○○	●●●○○
Versatility	Sensors
●●●●●	●●●●●

Drogo Dragon (J-20)

Speed	Air support
●●●●●	●●●●●
Stealth	Ground Support
●●●●○	●●●○○
Maneuverability	Endurance
●●●○○	●●●○○
Versatility	Sensors
●●●●○	●●●●○

Sammy & Sofia Strike Eagle (F-15E)

Speed	Air support
●●●●○	●●●●○
Stealth	Ground Support
●●○○○	●●●●●
Maneuverability	Endurance
●●●○○	●●●●○
Versatility	Sensors
●●●●●	●●●●○

Melvin & Milton Migs (F-5)

Speed	Air support
●●●○○	●●●○○
Stealth	Ground Support
●●○○○	●●●○○
Maneuverability	Endurance
●●●○○	●●○○○
Versatility	Sensors
●●●○○	●●○○○

About the Author - Meet Taylor Fox

Taylor is a former fighter pilot with over a decade of experience in The U.S. Air Force flying the F-22 and F-16. Taylor's love for aviation started at a young age, as he looped through the skies with his former fighter-pilot grandfather, Papa Jack. When he's not writing books, Taylor can be found flying across the world as an airline pilot or hanging out with his nephews, convincing them to become pilots someday. So buckle up, put on your aviator goggles, and join Taylor, callsign Chop, on a high-flying adventure with the AeroSquad!

About the Illustrator - Meet Celina Milla

El Salvador native Celina Milla is the designer behind the beloved character designs in AeroSquad. Still a kid at heart, Celina has worked closely with children organizations throughout her life. Combining Taylor's keen eye for representing aircraft accurately, and her commitment to creating characters that all kids would enjoy, the AeroSquad cartoons were born.

Aviation Glossary

Afterburners - Turbo boosters for jet engines. Extra fuel is injected into the exhaust creating a burst of flames out of the back of the jet, giving them a powerful speed boost!

Bandit - A known bad guy or enemy.

Bugout (Bugged out) - The act of quickly and urgently leaving a dangerous or challenging situation while flying.

Radar - A gadget that works like magical eyes in the sky. Radars send out invisible radio waves that bounce back to find things far away, similar to the sonar bats use!

Sonic boom - A loud noise, like thunder, caused when airplanes fly faster than the speed of sound and break the sound barrier.

Stealth - A cool trick that helps special airplanes become invisible to radars and sneak around the sky without being easily detected.

Sound barrier - A special speed limit for airplanes that is the speed of sound. If a plane breaks this speed limit, it creates a loud 'sonic boom' noise!

Stratosphere - The high layer of sky above most clouds with the ozone layer that protects Earth. The air is thin and very cold.

How good are your Pilot eyes? Answers:

1. Cat, page 22.   2. 16 birds.   3. Pedro Panther, page 5.   4. Magic, page 13.   5. Top right, page 7.   6. Page 23, over the mountain.

37

More from

The Adventures of AeroSquad

Coming soon
Sammy & Sofia Strike Eagles!

Coming soon
Pedro Panther takes on the Sky Bandits

Vicky Viper
& the Thunderchickens
Available NOW!

HardCover
2 Adventures in One!
Available NOW!

Join our Squad!

Stay connected with updates, bonus content, and more adventures from the "AeroSquad" series.

Bring the excitement home with official AeroSquad merch!

AeroSquad.Kids

AeroSquadKids.com